Welcome to The Pit!

The underground headquarters of the G.I. Joe Team is your new home. That's because you are about to become their newest member.

Your code name: Wiseguy

Your major talent: To think fast and make wise decisions under pressure.

Your assignment: Strategy Specialist.

A special G.I. Joe squad is about to go into action. The mission will not be an easy one. As Strategy Specialist, it will be up to you to make sure it is a *successful* one!

Follow the directions at the bottom of each page. Then make your decision about what to do next.

If you make the right decisions, the G.I. Joe Team will score a triumph over the forces of COBRA, and you will be recognized as a hero. If you make the wrong choices—you'll wish you never left The Pit!!

Good luck, soldier. Begin your mission on page 1.

THE EVERGLADES SWAMP TERROR

BY ERIC AFFABEE

BALLANTINE BOOKS • NEW YORK

RLI   VL: Grades 5 + up
      IL: Grades 6 + up

Copyright © 1986 by Hasbro, Inc.

G.I. JOE_{TM}: A trademark of Hasbro, Inc.
FIND YOUR FATE_{TM}: A trademark of Random House, Inc.

Library of Congress Catalog Card Number: 85-91214

ISBN 0-345-32986-4

Illustrated by David Henderson

Cover Art by Hector Garrido

Interior Design by Gene Siegel

Editorial Services by Parachute Press, Inc.

Manfactured in the United States of America

First Edition: February 1986

FIND YOUR FATE™

#5

G.I. JOE

THE EVERGLADES SWAMP TERROR

"What's the matter, Recondo—can't you move?" Deep Six yells. He gives Recondo a playful shove. "You've been out in the jungle so long, you can't walk—you can only swing on vines. Here—want a banana?"

"Give me a break, Deep Six," Recondo says with a scowl. "You've been on the ocean so long, your brain jumped ship!"

"It's zero-two hundred hours—the middle of the night," Lady Jaye complains. "What's the matter with Duke? Doesn't he know that even a G.I. Joe needs her beauty sleep?"

"Gung-Ho needs his beauty sleep, too," Deep Six mutters. "He needs about two hundred years! Ha ha!" Gung-Ho ignores him.

Joking through your yawns, you and five other members of the G.I. Joe Team make your way quickly through the second level of The Pit, to the Briefing Room. Why has Duke called an emergency meeting at this hour?

You push open the heavy door and step inside. Duke, Acting First Sergeant, is already seated at the head of the long conference table. And the grim look on his face tells you that the joking is over!

Turn to page 6.

1

You make a short search for Stoney, but he has disappeared into the swamps. You can picture him running off, a wide grin on his bearded face as he imagines you helpless on your own. But Recondo is along on this mission, and there is no better guide through swamp or jungle. "Look, the weeds bend back along here," he says, peering through the darkness. "The only way the wind could blow this way is if there's a clearing directly ahead. Let's go straight and see—"

KA-BLAAAAAAAAM!

A rifle shot!

Turn to page 16.

"Head for the Hovercraft now!" you shout to the others.

Gung-Ho pushes two COBRA guards aside and butts another one out of the way with his rifle handle. Recondo hits the dirt as automatic-rifle fire cuts a line through the tent above him. He crawls quickly toward the Hovercraft.

You start to make a run for it, but you immediately realize you've got to get past Major Bludd first!

Turn to page 85.

The old man grabs the ten-dollar bill with one quick motion of his long, bony fingers. The hand disappears back behind the counter. "I seem to recollect something, now that you mention it," he says, looking up for the first time.

"Well?" Gung-Ho asks menacingly.

"There were a coupla' fellas in uniforms through here a while back."

"How long ago?" you ask.

"Hmmm...a day or so," the old man says slowly. "Seems to me I heard tell they were doin' something in old Squirrely Jasper's cabin up in the mountains. You just go past town about a mile, turn right at the square boulder. Take Mule's Path up the mountain. You can't miss it."

The Joe Team is out the door before the store owner finishes talking. Your jeeps roar out of town, and a few minutes later you begin the climb up Mule's Path. You bump along the unpaved path for nearly half an hour, twisting your way slowly up the dry, brown mountainside.

"There's the cabin!" Lady Jaye cries.

You screech to a halt, leap quickly out of the jeeps, and use them for cover. Are COBRA guards holding your two buddies in this ramshackle mountain cabin?

Turn to page 24.

4

"Depth charge is operational," Cutter reports a few minutes later. "It's hard to assess the potential damage it could cause, Wiseguy. But we're pretty sure it could blow a hole in the fortress that can't be repaired."

"Let's hope we don't have to use it," you say thoughtfully. "Let's hope that the threat of it is enough."

"There's only one small problem with this plan," Cutter continues, hesitating, looking out to the tossing waves.

"A small problem?" you ask. "*How* small?"

"Well...in order to position the charge correctly, we've gotta be right on top of the fortress!"

Turn to page 26.

Duke nods a solemn greeting as you and five G.I. Joe Team members take your places around the conference table. The lights are dim and the air is heavy. You look around the table at your companions. The group is made up of Cutter, the former Coast Guardsman who always looks ill at ease on land; Gung-Ho, the wildest and toughest Marine; Deep Six, the best diver ever to put on a wetsuit; Recondo, an expert jungle fighter; and Lady Jaye, master spy.

Why have you six been called here in the middle of the night?

"I don't know whether to say good morning or good evening," Duke says, rubbing a hand through his short blond hair. "I only know there's nothing good about it." He closes the folder in front of him on the table and stands up.

"I've called this group together because we have a bit of a problem," he continues. "It involves two fellow team members." Duke's large hands press tightly against the back of his chair until the knuckles grow white.

"Torpedo and Trip-Wire are missing," he says quietly. "We have reason to believe they have been kidnapped by COBRA!"

Go on to page 7.

A shocked murmur echoes through the room. This time COBRA Command, the underground terrorist group determined to take over the world, has gone too far! *Nobody* messes with G.I. Joe!

Duke waits for the room to grow silent again. Then he explains: "These two team members were sent to the Florida Everglades on a top-secret mission. Some hot-shot army scientists built a new kind of Hovercraft, and they were real eager to have it tested out. So I sent Torpedo and Trip-Wire down to the swamps to give the thing a test drive."

"What happened?" Deep Six interrupts. "They drove the thing to Cuba?!"

Duke's face remains solemn. "We don't know," he says. "One hour after they arrived at their secret destination in the Everglades, we lost all radio contact with them. All attempts to get through to them failed. We knew that something was going on down there—but *what*?" Duke scowls. "Then, in the Communications Center, Breaker picked up a radio transmission...."

Turn to page 14.

Strong hands grab you just as you begin to plummet into the water. "Hey—this ain't no time for a swim!" Gung-Ho yells.

He pulls you to your feet and begins to drag you across the broken, bobbing deck. "The ... freighter ... it's...." You struggle to stop your head from spinning.

"The freighter has had it," Gung-Ho says, hurrying you across the deck. "But the *Whale* is hardly scratched."

He shoves you into the hatch of the G.I. Joe Hovercraft.

"Hey, Wiseguy, where've you been?" Cutter yells. You see that the others are safe inside the *Whale*.

"Let's get going!" you cry, your energy returning as you see that they're all safe.

With a roar, the *Whale* swoops off the sinking freighter and races over the tumbling waves.

"Uh-oh," Lady Jaye says. "We're being followed!"

Turn to page 27.

You follow Snow Job and Shipwreck up to the radar unit on the bridge. According to the beeping radar, six antiship missiles are plummeting over the waves, aimed directly at the freighter.

"No time to get out of the way. We've got to stand and fight 'em!" Snow Job yells.

"I'm punching up the missile-suppression systems now," Shipwreck says. "Our antimissile guns are guided by radar. We should be able to stop all six."

"And if we don't?" you ask hesitantly.

"If we don't," he replies, staring straight ahead at the radar screen, "we go *boom*."

Turn to page 21.

"Okay, Jaye, you've got a green light," you tell her.

"My favorite color," she says, snapping on her diving mask and grabbing her laser pistol. Before you can say anything else, she is over the side, diving down to help Deep Six.

You watch on the scanner as Deep Six continues to descend toward the underwater COBRA stronghold. He dives smoothly, with expert motions, seemingly unaware of the sharks that circle just above him.

The sharks turn away from him now as Lady Jaye approaches. They swim up to her, side by side, picking up speed as they descend effortlessly through the dark waters. Deep Six turns to watch. He seems to be waving Lady Jaye away. He seems upset, annoyed that she has entered the water.

The sharks approach her. She raises her laser—and *fires!*

One of the sharks appears to leap backward in the water. But you know it didn't leap. It was tossed back by the force of Jaye's laser. Dead. Deep Six continues to wave her away, gesturing frantically for her to leave.

Then the second shark, stunned for just a moment, attacks. It lunges toward Lady Jaye, grabbing her arm in its powerful jaws. The laser gun floats out of her grasp....

Turn to page 35.

11

Ramshackle wooden huts huddle under drooping trees where the sandy shoreline meets the edge of the Everglades jungle. You hear a baby crying in the nearest hut. A man pokes his head out. A few other men approach. Their clothing is torn and dirty. Some of them are carrying fishing poles.

They stare at you in silence. There are eight or ten of them blocking your way to the jungle. Gung-Ho raises his rifle, but you signal for him to put it back at his side.

"We're sorry to interrupt your day like this," you call out. "I guess you don't get many visitors down here."

A boy of about ten or eleven runs out of one of the huts to stare at you. He is barefoot and his shorts are ripped. He isn't wearing a shirt, and you can see all of his ribs. Obviously, he hasn't eaten much recently. A man, probably his father, shoves him and orders him back into the hut.

"What do you catch here?" you ask, struggling to make conversation.

"Mostly catfish. That's all," one of them says finally.

"How do they ever make a living fishing for catfish?" Cutter asks you.

"They don't," you reply. "Look at them."

"Hey—what do you want with us, huh?" one of the fishermen asks, menace in his voice.

....

Go on to page 13.

12

"Two of our buddies were down here a couple of days ago," Deep Six tells them. "Any of you recall seeing them?"

The fishermen begin to mutter among themselves. You study their narrow, drawn faces. They look nervous, but none of them seem willing to speak up. They just stand there, shaking their heads.

"We have information that they were right on this spot," Deep Six insists. "You mean to tell me that none of you saw them here?"

The fishermen stare back at you nervously. "We just fish. We don't see anything," one of them mutters, studying his fishing pole. The others nod in agreement.

Suddenly a tall man with a red beard and long, tangled red hair steps forward. His T-shirt is torn and tobacco-stained, and his sandals are tied together with string. "I saw your friends," he says, grinning. "How much is it worth to you to find them?"

Turn to page 48.

13

Duke presses a button on the intercom on the conference table. Breaker stumbles into the Briefing Room and gives Duke a limp salute. "Sorry. Not quite awake," he says with a yawn.

"Tell them about the transmission you picked up," Duke says.

"I have the transcript right here," Breaker says, holding up a sheet of yellow paper. "This radio transmission was intercepted yesterday at twenty hours. I traced it to the Everglades. The message is from a COBRA agent." Breaker reads the transcript of the intercepted message:

"'CG 12-24B, reporting to HQ. Location 33-X, Code 5-3-7. Have collected quarry. Both birds in the bag. The bus has changed hands. Await travel plans. Repeat. Quarry has been collected. Please advise. Over.'"

Duke thanks Breaker and tells him he can go back to bed. Then he turns to you and your team members. "That message is pretty clear," he says. "And your job is clear, too. You've got to get down there and rescue Torpedo and Trip-Wire. And you've got to get that experimental Hovercraft back in our hands!"

"What's COBRA doing down in the Everglades?" Lady Jaye asks.

"Good question," Duke replies ominously. "I'm sure you'll find out soon enough!"

Go on to page 15.

14

Okay, Wiseguy—you're the Strategy Specialist. You know that it's up to you to come up with a plan to rescue your kidnapped buddies and retrieve the top-secret Hovercraft from COBRA. Quickly, you come up with two strategies:

STRATEGY #1
The G.I. Joe freighter is in the Atlantic off the Florida coast. The freighter is heavily armed, a well-equipped fortress for coastal waters. You fly to the freighter and use it as a base, reaching the swamps by Hovercraft with the freighter's weapons ready to back you up. Major disadvantage: You lose time by traveling first to the freighter, time which may be critical.

STRATEGY #2
You fly by helicopter directly to the spot of the COBRA transmission in the Everglades. This may enable you to make a fast rescue—get in and get out! It may also enable you to take the COBRA by surprise. Major disadvantage: You will not be able to carry heavy arms, and you will have no heavily armed fortress to offer backup support.
Which strategy will you choose?

....

Strategy 1? Turn to page 42.
Strategy 2? Turn to page 32.

15

You realize immediately that it was Lady Jaye who fired the rifle. Recondo drops to his knees and picks up something from the wet sand. You throw a light onto it.

"A snake!" Gung-Ho cries. "Lady Jaye shot its head off!"

"It's not just any· snake," Recondo says, a tremble in his voice. "It's a black mamba! You just saved my life, Jaye."

"I try to earn my pay," she says quietly. "Now see if you can guide us *away* from the deadly snakes instead of toward them, Recondo."

"The only deadly snakes *I* want to find are COBRAs!" Gung-Ho says, as you follow Recondo through the swamp.

You don't have far to travel to find what Gung-Ho is after. Just as Recondo thought, there is a clearing several hundred yards ahead of you—and in the clearing you see two small, yellow campfires glowing in front of low, black tents. Behind the tents in the deep shadows you can make out a few black Hovercrafts with red insignias on the front.

You have found the COBRA CAMP!

Turn to page 79.

"Arizona?! They took Trip-Wire and Torpedo to Arizona?" Cutter cries, as surprised as the rest of you.

"It could be a fake," Lady Jaye warns. "It may be a COBRA trick to get us out of the area."

Or... it may be the truth. Your two comrades might be long gone from the Florida coastal waters—and their lives may depend on you. You must decide what to do. Do you think the transmission is a fake? Or should you be on your way immediately to Arizona?

Stay in Florida? Turn to page 46.
Go to Arizona? Turn to page 57.

17

"It's a trap!" Lady Jaye cries.

"What a smart lady!" Stoney says with a wide smile. "Some fellas gave us these fancy rifles and paid us more than we make in a year to keep you guys out of the swamps. And that's just what we aim to do. Drop your weapons!"

The fishermen quickly surround you. A quick count tells you there are nine of them and only six of you. The ocean is behind you. No way to retreat. The swamps begin a few hundred feet ahead of you.

"You're right pretty," Stoney says, walking up to Lady Jaye and looking her up and down. "Maybe we'll keep you alive a bit longer than the others. Whaddaya say, guys?"

The fishermen laugh and whistle as Lady Jaye scowls and stares back at them defiantly.

Gung-Ho leans over and whispers, "Come on, Wiseguy—we can take 'em. They don't look so tough!"

You have only a second or two to decide. Try to fight them even though the odds are stacked against you? Or wait for a better moment to escape?

Wait? Turn to page 28.
Fight them? Turn to page 52.

18

"The alligator!" you yell to Gung-Ho. He gives you a quizzical look as he blasts at two attacking COBRAs. Then he catches on to your idea.

"Okay, alligator—freedom time!" Gung-Ho yells, shoving aside the COBRA guard who is grappling with the animal's chain.

The alligator snaps its massive jaws as the guard falls backward, jagged teeth closing on the screaming COBRA's leg.

You pull at the chain. Cutter tosses you his laser knife. You catch it in midair, activate it, and a few seconds later the alligator is free.

"Go get 'em!" you cry.

But the ungrateful alligator attacks *you*!

Turn to page 45.

"We'll be back by dawn. I promise," you tell Cutter and Recondo, after doing all you can to ease their pain.

Evening descends quickly. A thick fog drifts down over the shoreline. Strange animal cries waft down from the darkening trees of the Everglades.

You, Gung-Ho, Lady Jaye, and Deep Six leave the sandy strip of shore and step into the tangled vines and jutting roots of the swamp.

"Stop right there!" a voice calls in the darkness.

COBRA soldiers surround you, stepping quickly from behind tall weeds and sloping trees. "Drop your rifles," a COBRA guard yells, and you realize you have no choice but to obey. "It was good of you to signal your arrival with all that gunfire," the COBRA guard leader says sarcastically.

Why is this area so important to COBRA? Why are so many COBRA soldiers stationed here? What COBRA secrets do these dark swamps hide?

Sadly, they will remain secrets. As the COBRA rifles ring out you realize you will receive no answers to your questions in this adventure. Here in the dark, fog-filled swamps, this adventure has come to its

END

KA-BLAAAAM! KA-BLAAAAAM!

The soft roar of the ocean waves is drowned out by the explosions when the *Jane*'s 30mm-gatling fire clashes head-on with an incoming missile.

"Two...three...four..."

You count the explosions. Six explosions will mean you've knocked out all six missiles.

"...Five...and...six! Hoooorrraaaay!" The freighter rings with laughter and cries of relief.

You turn to Cutter. "Someone's determined to keep us out of this area."

"COBRA doesn't exactly have the welcome mat out," Cutter says somberly.

"But *why* are they so desperate to keep us away? It can't just be the Hovercraft they stole or Torpedo and Trip-Wire," you say.

"Hey—I'm picking up a strange transmission up here on the radio," Snow Job calls from the radio cabin. "I think you guys better listen in on this!"

Turn to page 34.

Wait! What is that roar from the water?

"I don't believe it!" you cry.

It's the *Whale*—a G.I. Joe Hovercraft!

Its guns blazing, the *Whale* roars right up onto the beach and plows into the center of the astounded COBRA guards.

"Hey—Shipwreck!" you yell, recognizing your smiling buddy. "This is what I call good timing!"

Shipwreck tosses you and your teammates weapons as he continues to pursue the fleeing Crimson Guards. "This is the way they do it in the movies, ain't it?" he cries.

The Hovercraft roars over the sand, and the Crimson Guards scatter into the swamp, running in all directions. "Jump in!" Shipwreck yells, triumphantly waving a rifle in the air as he guides the *Whale* with one hand. "Let's follow 'em to their camp!"

A few seconds later the *Whale* is rumbling over jutting vines and roots, through wet sand hills and watery inlets, carrying you and the G.I. Joe Team toward the COBRA camp.

Up ahead, you see the small camp in a clearing. "There seem to be only a few guards left in camp!" you say in surprise. "Either this is too good to be true—or we're heading into a trap!"

Turn to page 54.

There is no sign of life coming from the primitive cabin built of logs and desert clay. One window, its glass shattered years before and never replaced, offers a glimpse—into darkness.

Footprints up to the rotted door indicate that someone has been here recently. But the tire tracks that lead *away* from the cabin and back down Mule's Path appear to be fresher than those leading *up* to it.

"Looks real quiet," you say. "Too quiet. Ready your weapons—and let's go in!"

Turn to page 37.

You peer into the Hovercraft's view screen and watch the black tank, its red COBRA insignia growing bigger and bigger as it closes the gap between you.

"Here they come," says Lady Jaye as missile launchers emerge from the front of the *Ferret*.

"Well, it's been fun," Recondo says with a grim smile.

"At least I won't have to spend any more time landlocked in The Pit," Deep Six adds.

The COBRAs launch their missiles.... You close your eyes...

...and Trip-Wire activates the antimissile guns on the back of the Hovercraft!

BAAAARRROOOOOOM!

The COBRA *Ferret* disappears in a fiery blaze.

You look back into the view screen. There is no one following you now.

Cutter grins at Deep Six. "Looks like you're headed for The Pit after all."

You're still too shaken up to join in the joking. "Trip-Wire, why didn't you tell me this new craft had antimissile guns on it?" you demand angrily.

"What?" he replies innocently. "And spoil the surprise ending for you?"

THE END

25

You know the task ahead is dangerous, maybe even deadly, but there's no choice but to proceed. You've got to position the freighter directly over the COBRA fortress, lower the depth charge, then speed out of its range without being detected by the COBRAs inside the underwater structure.

You stand beside Shipwreck as he mans the wheel, carefully maneuvering the freighter. "Easy, easy," Cutter says from the other side of the small cabin, his eyes on the scanner.

"Cutter, what are the odds that you'll come out a hero for dreaming up this plan?" you ask as Shipwreck feverishly guides the ship.

"I'm not a gambling man," Cutter says quietly. "Hold 'er steady, Shipwreck. We're in position, guys."

You hit the controls. "Lowering the depth charge now," you say, your voice a bit shaky. "Depth charge is in the water now...and..."

A momentary silence.

More silence.

Your heart begins to pound against your chest.

"Hey—they've spotted us!" Shipwreck cries in alarm.

Turn to page 38.

COBRA Hovercrafts—six of them—have swooped up from the underground fortress and are in close pursuit. "Turn the *Whale* around!" you order as COBRA guns roar out a deafening blast. "Activate the missile launchers!"

"They're in too close," Cutter warns. "We can't use missiles. We'll blow *ourselves* up, too!"

"You're right," you quickly agree. "Okay, we'll do it the old-fashioned way. Get to the gun turrets. We'll shoot 'em out of the water!"

A few seconds later your guns are rattling back at the pursuing COBRA crafts. "Six-to-one odds—that's better than in Las Vegas!" Recondo yells over the roar of weaponfire.

KA-RRROOOOOM!

"We're down to *five*-to-one odds!" you yell happily as a COBRA Hovercraft explodes in a fiery burst. "Keep shooting!"

The COBRAs put up a good chase, but G.I. Joe determination and battleskill are too much for them. A few minutes later the six COBRA Hovercrafts have all been blasted out of the water.

"Good shooting!" you say. "We suddenly seem to be alone out here."

"No we're not!" Cutter yells. "There's one more!"

Turn to page 82.

27

"Drop your weapons," you tell the other Joe Team members. "Don't try anything crazy. They've got us."

Gung-Ho groans and gives you an angry stare, but he throws down his rifle. You and the others toss your weapons to the sand.

"Very wise, very wise," Stoney says, gloating. "Now, if you big-shot soldiers would care to follow us poor fishermen...."

He and his companions enjoy a good laugh as they force you at riflepoint to follow them. You find yourselves walking along the narrow shoreline between the ocean and the thick trees of the Everglade swamps.

"Where are you taking us?" Lady Jaye asks.

"We're takin' you to camp," Stoney says, leering. "COBRA camp!"

Just as he says these words, you hear a loud cry—and out of the tangled swamps steps a unit of COBRA's elite Crimson Guards, their automatic rifles poised and ready!

Turn to page 64.

"Let me dive down there—" Deep Six begins.

"I *knew* that would be part of your plan!" you say. "Even a COBRA fortress can't keep you out of the water, Deep Six."

"But I *know* my plan will work," he protests. "Look at the top right quadrant of the fortress. Our sensors show that the heat level is higher in that area. That has to be the power supply for the fortress."

"So?" Cutter asks impatiently.

"I'll dive down to the fortress, locate the power supply, and set off an explosive device. This plan can't fail. With the power supply gone, the COBRAs will be forced out."

"They'll have to come to the surface," Shipwreck says, catching on to Deep Six's idea.

"And we'll be waiting for them. We'll capture them and take back Torpedo and Trip-Wire. What do you say, Wiseguy?"

All eyes turn to you. Which plan will you choose?

....

Cutter's plan to threaten COBRA with a depth charge? Turn to page 39.

Deep Six's plan to dive down and blow up their power source? Turn to page 49.

"Okay, we'll do it now," you say. "Let's wipe 'em out!"

The six of you attack the camp, your automatic rifles blazing. The COBRA soldiers are taken by surprise. Three of them hit the dirt, fatally wounded before anyone has a chance to cry out.

Your attack is short—and successful.

More COBRAs come rushing out of the tents, but they are mowed down by your weaponfire. You realize that there are fewer than a dozen of the enemy in this camp.

"We've won. Now search the tents!" you cry.

Deep Six and Recondo run from tent to tent, jumping over the bodies of fallen COBRA.

"All empty," Deep Six reports back a few minutes later. "No sign of our buddies." He shrugs.

"This must be the wrong camp," you say unhappily.

"Yes, it *is* the wrong camp—for *you*!" a voice calls from behind you.

Turn to page 58.

You tell Duke you'd rather go directly to the Everglades.

"Good luck—and hurry back," Duke says grimly. He turns and walks quickly out of the room. The other team members turn to you to hear your strategy.

"Let's wake up Wild Bill and tell him to get the *Dragonfly* helicopter operational," you tell them. "COBRA isn't going to stay in the swamps any longer than they have to. We've got to get down there as fast as we can."

"I'll second that!" Lady Jaye says.

Turn to page 69.

"What's that barreling toward us?" Trip-Wire cries.

"Ha ha! It's not the *Queen Mary*!" Cutter yells happily, waving his arms wildly. "It's the G.I. Joe freighter!"

"Hey—nice of you guys to drop by!" you call into the Hovercraft radio.

"Well, we happened to be in the neighborhood," a voice replies in your headphones. It's Shipwreck. "But I see you already have company."

"Not for long!" you yell back.

The freighter opens fire on the COBRA Hovercrafts, but they are already making a fast retreat through the tall, choppy waves.

KA-BLAAAAAAM!

A *Water Moccasin* goes up in a blaze of red and yellow flames, then sinks out of sight into the ocean.

"A fireworks show!" Gung-Ho yells. "What next?"

"What next?" you repeat. "I'll tell you—next comes a happy ending!"

As the COBRA race away in defeat, you smile at your rescued comrades and direct the Hovercraft toward the freighter, which will soon be carrying you home.

THE END

You and the others rush to the radio cabin to listen to the transmission. "This seems to be a COBRA wavelength," Snow Job says. "It's not on a normal band. I accidentally cut into it just now."

You listen carefully:

"COBRA 12, this is CG 49. COBRA 12, this is CG 49. Please scramble transmission now. Over."

There are a few seconds of static. Then the COBRA agent continues. The message is obviously being scrambled after your interception, for you hear it loud and clear:

"We have the Hovercraft in tow and have taken custody of two—repeat two—enemy soldiers of lesser rank. As ordered, I have taken the prisoners to Area 234-D, where they are being held pending further orders. Please respond. Over." The radio goes silent.

"Snow Job, were you able to trace that transmission?" you ask eagerly.

Snow Job looks up from his control board with a puzzled expression on his weatherworn face. "I traced it, all right," he tells you. "The transmission came from the Arizona desert!"

Turn to page 17.

"I'm not sure I want to see this," Cutter says as you watch Lady Jaye struggle to free herself from the shark. But you can't take your eyes off the scanner. You watch, mesmerized, as Deep Six retrieves her laser pistol. He raises it . . . and fires.

He fires again.

The shark freezes. It jerks back its head, allowing Lady Jaye to pull her arm out with a quick motion.

Another blast of the laser pistol misses. But Deep Six's next shot is a fatal one. The shark seems to wither. It floats in place. It will not attack again.

You watch as Deep Six swims over to examine Lady Jaye's arm. "Whew! She must be okay," you say with relief. "She's waving him away."

"Either she's okay, or she's *nuts*!" Cutter says. "They're continuing down to the fortress!"

You watch as they dive farther down. And as you watch you suddenly see the COBRA rocket launchers move into place on the fortress roof.

You realize immediately what has happened. The shots from Lady Jaye's laser pistol alerted the COBRAs!!

Turn to page 44.

Wild Bill makes the *Dragonfly* spin—and drop. The COBRA missiles roar above you, missing by only a few yards.

"That's a little too close for comfort!" Wild Bill cries.

"Fire Two!" you yell.

A second missile speeds from the *Dragonfly*...

...and hits its target!

The COBRA jet becomes a twirling fireball. It plunges into the ocean and disappears beneath the green-blue waters.

"And the score is two to nothing, in our favor," Cutter says with a grin.

"But it's only the top of the first," you tell him.

"I'm letting you passengers off now," Wild Bill says as he brings the *Dragonfly* down. "I hope you've got round-trip tickets."

"This is *my* ticket home!" Gung-Ho yells, raising his rifle.

The chopper lands with a jolt on the sandy shoreline. Sea gulls squawk and flap out of your way. With a salute to Wild Bill, you leap out of the hatch, followed by your companions. You're all glad to be on solid ground, even if it's wet sand. But wait a minute! This part of the Everglades is supposed to be uninhabited, and you seem to be in some kind of village!

Turn to page 12.

Rifles in hand, you burst through the open doorway.

"What the—" Gung-Ho stops short.

The cabin is deserted. There isn't even a stick of furniture. On the floor in the corner you see a tape player and a radio transmitter. You rewind the tape and play it back:

"COBRA 12, this is CG 49...COBRA 12, this is CG 49. Please scramble transmission now...."

"A tape recording!" Cutter cries angrily. "We've been tricked!"

"I'd better use this transmitter to radio The Pit," you say, shaking your head unhappily. A few seconds later you make contact with Duke back at The Pit.

Duke does not sound pleased to hear from you. "You guys completely missed the action," he snaps. "Torpedo and Trip-Wire managed to battle their way out of the Everglades without your help. But COBRA kept the Hovercraft. I hope you all have real embarrassed looks on your faces."

"Yeah," you say uncomfortably. "Guess we should head back to The Pit now."

"You do that," Duke says sarcastically. "That is, if you're sure you don't want to fly to Maine or maybe Oregon first!"

THE END

"Set off the depth charge!" Cutter yells, his voice high with panic.

"No—it isn't down yet! We'll blow ourselves out of the water!" you tell him.

"It's our only chance!" Cutter insists. "Blow it up! Blow it up! If we've been spotted, we're doomed anyway!!"

"Setting off the depth charge now would be *suicide*!" Shipwreck protests. "It's just too risky—even for us. We've got to see what COBRA does first!"

Quick, Wiseguy—you have less than a second to decide!

Set off the depth charge? Turn to page 68.
Wait to see what COBRA does? Turn to page 70.

"Okay, Cutter, we'll give your plan the nod," you decide. "How big a charge can we lower from this crate?" you ask Shipwreck.

"Big enough," he says quietly.

"And how long will it take for the charge to land in an advantageous location?" you ask him.

"Not long," he answers.

"Long enough for us to get out of the way if we decide to set it off?"

"Maybe," he replies.

"Shipwreck, you've been real informative," you say with a scowl. You turn away from him. "Let's lower the boom on these COBRAs. Maneuver the ship into position—and let's hope our explosive little visitor gets down to *them* before they send a few up to *us!*"

Turn to page 5.

"I say we go in," Gung-Ho demands.

"Not yet," you say. "But let's get close to the real thing and keep an eye on our friend Bludd."

Recondo leads the Joe Team to a spot outside the real camp where, with Cutter standing guard, you all pass a long, fitful night.

As the sun rises over the swamp and yellow sunlight filters down through the thick trees, Cutter wakes you. COBRA Commander's evil henchman Major Bludd is emerging from the center tent, adjusting his eye patch. Minutes later four COBRA guards drag Torpedo and Trip-Wire from their tent and tie them to a wooden post.

A roar shakes the trees. A black and red Hovercraft, a COBRA *Water Moccasin*, speeds over the marshy sand to the center of the camp. You watch as the Baroness steps out of the *Water Moccasin*, followed by COBRA Commander himself!

Turn to page 76.

A few miles off the Florida coast, in shimmering blue waters under a fat orange sun, the G.I. Joe freighter, the *Jane*, cruises lazily, patrolling the silent, seemingly empty waters. The long, narrow ship moves slowly, bobbing on the waves, puffs of black smoke wafting up from its archaic steampipes.

But you know that there is nothing archaic about the antimissile radar equipment and laser weaponry of the innocent-looking ship. The missile-equipped *Jane* is a floating fortress, capable of lightning attack and able to defend against practically anything.

You jump out of the skycopter that carried the G.I. Joe Team down to the freighter and run forward to greet two of the freighter crew, Shipwreck and Snow Job.

"How long have you guys been on vacation down here?" you ask.

"Hey, what's with you, Wiseguy?" Shipwreck asks. "You think we're just down here to catch the rays? We got enough to keep us busy."

"Looks to me like you've got a pretty good tan, Shipwreck," Cutter says, joining the conversation.

"Vacation's over!" a voice calls from the bridge. "We've got incoming missilefire!"

Turn to page 9.

"Deep Six can take care of himself," you tell them. Lady Jaye tosses down the diving suit, disappointed. "Look—the sharks are turning away. They seem to be afraid to come near the fortress."

"They're not as dumb as they look," Recondo says, as relieved as everyone else.

Deep Six gives a wave as he reaches the near wall of the COBRA underwater fortress. Then he disappears from view, slipping behind the fortress to locate the power source.

"Nothing like a little suspense to get the heart pounding," Cutter says. "Poor old Deep Six'll wish he had the sharks to fight if the COBRAs catch him back there."

Everyone stares at the scanner screen in silence. But there is nothing to see. Deep Six is truly on his own now.

You wait... and wait.

The only sounds are the cries of gulls overhead and the crash of waves against the sides of the freighter.

Finally, Deep Six emerges from behind the fortress. You see at once that he is no longer carrying the explosives. Now all he has to do is get safely back to the freighter before the charge goes off.

Turn to page 53.

43

The victory over the sharks was G.I. Joe's final victory in these Florida waters. For now you are all sitting ducks for the COBRA weapons.

Deep Six and Lady Jaye watch helplessly from the ocean depths as the COBRA rocket launchers send their deadly rockets up to the surface and to the freighter.

You stare at the scanner, realizing you are watching your own doom. Your only solace is the thought that this is not the final battle against the evil forces of COBRA. There are other G.I. Joe Teams who will continue the fight. And you have no doubt that G.I. Joe—eventually—will be *victorious*!

THE END

You roll to the side as the massive creature charges. It misses you and knocks over a COBRA guard who was sneaking up behind you. The guard screams in agony as the alligator's jaws close around his waist. He struggles to push the beast off, but the alligator is too heavy to be pushed. You look away as the fierce animal finishes off its prey.

COBRAs scatter in all directions. The alligator slithers quickly after another guard, who trips and falls, and scrambles away from the crashing jaws.

"To the Hovercraft! Fast!" you cry, eager to take advantage of the confusion the gigantic alligator is causing.

A few seconds later you and the rest of the G.I. Joe Team have piled into the experimental Hovercraft.

"Which way, Wiseguy?" Trip-Wire asks, his hands moving over the controls. "You'd better decide quick. They're gonna be comin' after us!"

Sure enough, you hear the roar of COBRA *Water Moccasins* behind you. "Head for the ocean!" Cutter yells. "We've got to get back to the freighter! Then we can blast 'em out of the water!"

"No—we'll be an easy target in the ocean," Recondo protests. "Let's try to lose 'em in the swamps!"

....

You decide, Wiseguy.
Head for the ocean? Turn to page 55.
Play hide-and-seek in the swamps? Turn to page 66.

45

"I'm more than a little suspicious about this radio transmission," you tell your fellow team members. "The timing is just too perfect."

"Yeah," Cutter agrees. "Why did the COBRA agent wait until five minutes after we arrived on the freighter to send his message?"

"And why wasn't the message scrambled from the point of origin?" Lady Jaye asks. "Because they *wanted* us to hear it and understand it," she finishes, answering her own question.

"We're staying here," you decide. "Trip-Wire and Torpedo aren't in Arizona. They're right here in Florida, and we're going to find them!"

"Hey, Wiseguy, Cutter—get up here!" It's Shipwreck calling from the radar cabin. "You're not going to believe this!!"

Go on to page 47.

"It's a good thing this freighter is equipped with an antiradar camouflage screen," Shipwreck says as you pile into the small cabin. "Take a look at what's almost directly beneath us."

You struggle to make out the image on the video screen. "Can you focus the scanner any better?" you ask. "It appears to be some kind of structure on the ocean floor, but I can't...."

The operator works the dials to focus the scanner.

"It's—it's some kind of fortress," Cutter says, his voice filled with surprise. "The sensors show that—I don't believe this!—it's built of solid steel!"

"Appears to be heavily armed. We're picking up rocket launchers...missiles...the works," Shipwreck adds grimly.

"It's about the size of a city block," Cutter adds, shaking his head. "It's fully manned, too. The sensors show there could be as many as two hundred to three hundred people down there. Wow!" He lets out a whistle of disbelief.

"*Wow* is right," you agree. "A COBRA fortress on the bottom of the Atlantic, less than two miles off the Florida coast. Torpedo and Trip-Wire must have accidentally discovered it—and *that's why they were kidnapped*!"

Turn to page 74.

47

The other fishermen tell him to shut up, but the tall, red-bearded man turns and stares them down. Then he walks toward you, tossing his pole to the ground. "My name's Stoney," he says. "You'll have to forgive my friends. They ain't used to company. And we've had a lot of company in recent days."

"What do you mean?" Gung-Ho asks suspiciously.

"Guys in funny-lookin' uniforms. Some kinda soldiers, I guess," Stoney says. "And I saw your buddies, too. Drivin' some kinda fancy boat."

"Where are they? Can you take us to them?" Cutter asks.

"Yep," Stoney says, grinning again.

The other fishermen start to argue and protest, but he ignores them. "Like I said," Stoney tells you, "it'll cost you. How's five hundred?"

"Five hundred dollars?" you ask.

"I'll guide you right to the camp they set up," Stoney says. "It ain't easy bein' a fisherman these days, y'know. That's why I like to moonlight as a guide." He laughs.

You stare at him, trying to decide what to do. There's a look of danger in his eyes. Is he planning to lead you into a trap? Or can he really take you to your kidnapped buddies? What will he and his friends do if you turn him down?

....

Do you choose to pay him and hire him as a guide? Turn to page 84.

Or do you choose to set off on your own? Turn to page 72.

48

"Okay, Deep Six," you say, deciding quickly, "I can't keep you out of the water. Go ahead. Dive down and see if you can give them a little scare."

"They won't know what hit them," he says with a grin.

"Just get back up here quickly," you tell him. "And if you detect any sign that you've been spotted, ditch the explosives and save yourself."

You turn and see that Deep Six hasn't heard a word you've said. He's already climbing into his diving suit. Gung-Ho and Cutter prepare the explosive charge he will carry with him. "The blast will go off three minutes after you plant the explosives and activate the timer," Cutter tells Deep Six. "Does that give you enough time?"

"Gives me enough time to do a little scuba diving and take a vacation down there," Deep Six boasts.

"At least he's not overconfident," Lady Jaye says and smiles.

You smile, too, but you really don't feel like it. This plan is a little too daring, even for your tastes. And the chances of it succeeding, you realize, are slim. You watch Deep Six slip on his diving mask—maybe for the last time....

....

Turn to page 62.

49

The roar of the explosion is followed by a deafening cracking sound as the deck of the G.I. Joe freighter is ripped apart by the blast. The deck breaks apart beneath you. You grab at a railing, but it flies from your grasp.

"We're going down!" someone yells. "We've been cut in half!"

You struggle to pull yourself to your feet, but as you arise the deck tilts up, tossing you back down. You hit your head against a railing. You sink to your knees. You are sliding...sliding... about to slide off the tilted, broken deck into the rolling, turbulent waters....

Turn to page 8.

You look at the fishermen nervously training their rifles on you. You decide that maybe Gung-Ho is right. "Okay," you say quietly, "let's go get 'em!"

You dive for the ground as their automatic rifles ring out. You grab a fishing pole and, pulling yourself up into a crouch, swing the pole into a fisherman's stomach.

He cries out in pain, and his rifle drops from his hand. You dive for it, and for a few desperate moments you and he scramble on the wet sand. Then Gung-Ho joins the fight, pulling the fisherman off you. You grab the rifle and begin firing at the fishermen.

The crashing of the waves against the shore is drowned out by riflefire. Suddenly Cutter drops to the ground and cries out in pain. *"I've been shot!"*

But there's no time to reach Cutter. You roll out of the way as a volley of riflefire drills a line in the sand....

Turn to page 65.

BA-RA-ROOOOOOOOOOOOOOOOM!

The explosion is more powerful than you had expected. You reach down and pull Deep Six onto the deck just as the charge goes off. The freighter rocks and spins as the ocean waters are split and tossed by the powerful blast.

Deep Six tears off his mask. He gasps for breath. "I think it worked," he says, grinning, as the freighter continues to be pushed and pulled crazily in the swelling, churned-up waters.

"So far, so good," you say. "Steady the boat!" you call to Shipwreck in the control cabin. "How are we going to fight COBRAs if we're all seasick?"

"You landlubbers have to learn to take a little turbulence," Shipwreck calls down.

"Here come the COBRAs!" Cutter yells.

Chased from their underwater stronghold, the bewildered, angered COBRAs bob to the surface. Some of them manage to grab diving suits before fleeing; others cling to damaged Hovercrafts and underwater crafts. Bodies float to the surface, too. The explosion has taken its toll....

Your eyes scan the water, searching for Torpedo and Trip-Wire.

Turn to page 88.

"BLAAAAM! BLAAAAM!"

The Joe Team opens fire on the startled COBRA guards. "We've caught 'em napping!" Gung-Ho yells. "Let's go get 'em!"

The battle is short and triumphant. The COBRAs don't stand a chance.

When the smoke has cleared, you leap out of the *Whale* and head for the tent where Torpedo and Trip-Wire are tied up.

"Hey, what took you so long?" Torpedo asks as you and Deep Six untie him.

"We spent a little time on the beach working on our tans," Deep Six answers.

Shipwreck rolls the Hovercraft right up to the tent. "Hey," he says, "we're working hard because you guys decided to take a Florida vacation. Now I suppose you'll want to hitch a ride with me back to the freighter?"

"No way," Trip-Wire replies. He points to the experimental Hovercraft at the edge of the camp. "We're going back first class—and Wiseguy is going to be our first passenger!"

Turn to page 86.

"Head for the ocean!" you cry to Trip-Wire as he maneuvers the big Hovercraft through the tangled trees, over vines and jutting roots, roaring over the treacherous, swampy ground. "They'll never be able to catch up to us on open waters!"

"Here's hopin'," Trip-Wire calls back.

"You tested this baby, Trip-Wire," Cutter breaks in. "You should know what she can do on open water."

"Well...we were rudely interrupted," Trip-Wire says as the Hovercraft splashes over a watery inlet, bumps over a bog, and races through tall weeds. "We didn't exactly get a chance to test—"

KA-BRRRROOOOOM!

Weaponfire from the four COBRA *Water Moccasin*s pursuing you shakes the Hovercraft. It spins around, out of control. *"We've been hit!"* Lady Jaye calls from the rear hatch.

Trip-Wire struggles to regain control of the Hovercraft. It is still spinning wildly as it plunges into ocean waters. The COBRAs are right behind you now.

KA-BRRRROOOOOM!

Another powerful blast sends the Hovercraft tumbling in the tall, dark waves. "Gotta get it straightened out!" Trip-Wire yells, but his voice is filled with doubt....

Turn to page 75.

"Hey, look at all the orange trees!" Lady Jaye says. The dawning sun is a dark red ball on the horizon as you fly low over Florida orange groves. "It looks just like a picture postcard."

"We won't be sending any postcards on this trip," you tell her, realizing you're close to your destination. The swamps of the Everglades stretch out below.

"Hey, we've got two planes approaching from the south," Wild Bill interrupts, "and they're not coming to say 'Welcome to Florida!'"

You look out into the pink morning clouds and see two black fighter jets coming toward you. "COBRA *Rattler*s!" you cry, recognizing the red COBRA insignia on the wings.

Wild Bill hits the controls, and the chopper climbs as the COBRA *Rattler*s open fire. "Hey, whatever happened to the Friendly Skies?" he mutters, swerving the *Dragonfly* out of the way of incoming missilefire. "What's your plan now, Wiseguy?"

The *Dragonfly* is armed with its *own* missiles. Should you tell Wild Bill to try to fight off the COBRA attack planes? Or should you and the other team members bail out of the *Dragonfly*? You're only a few miles from the spot of the COBRA radio transmission.

. . . .

Bail out? Turn to page 78.
Fight them off? Turn to page 61.

The flight to Arizona is turbulent and storm-tossed. But when you land in Tucson, the sun is beaming and the air is hot and dry. "Just the way it's supposed to be," Deep Six proclaims.

"I guess it's okay if you like this sort of place," Recondo grumbles. "I was sort of looking forward to the Everglades myself."

"This isn't a pleasure trip," you remind them. "We've come a long way to get Trip-Wire and Torpedo. Let's hope this isn't a wild-goose chase."

The six of you pile into two jeeps on loan from the Marines and head out toward the desert. Gung-Ho is showing off his new assault rifle to Lady Jaye. "This ain't standard issue," he tells her, slapping the rifle butt. "This is a 5.56 mm rifle-machine gun. Takes a 64-round magazine, shoots 420 rounds a minute, and I can feed her in three seconds flat."

Lady Jaye looks less than impressed. "Let's hope we don't have to use it," she says quietly.

You're thinking the same thing as you ponder the map given to you by Snow Job. The small red *X* he's drawn—fifty miles outside of Tucson—indicates the spot of the radio transmission.

What is waiting for you at the spot of the *X*?

....

Turn to page 83.

57

You spin around and stare into the masked face of COBRA Commander! Beside him stands his evil henchman, Major Bludd. You see quickly that the whole camp is now surrounded by COBRA soldiers, their rifles aimed at you and your companions, their fingers poised, awaiting the command to fire.

"You made so much noise attacking our little decoy camp, we just had to come and investigate," COBRA Commander says sarcastically. "What a pity you did not choose to visit our *real* camp. I believe a couple of your friends are staying there. Ha ha!"

Your eyes survey the whole camp. You look desperately for a way to escape. "Allow me to thank you for the wonderful new Hovercraft you decided to donate to the COBRA cause," COBRA Commander continues.

The sound of his laughter is drowned out by the roar of COBRA rifles. As you fall you know that you have failed. But you also know that the G.I. Joe Team will be back to fight again— and G.I. Joe *will prevail*!

THE END

As the COBRA guards struggle to drag the alligator forward, Major Bludd prepares a syringe. "These G.I. jokers will help us test the serum, COBRA Commander."

COBRA Commander explodes in a fit of anger. "The *serum*! The *serum*! How many weeks have you wasted down here working on that blasted serum!!?"

Major Bludd chooses to ignore his commander's anger. "The serum will work," he says calmly. "You will see for yourself that as soon as I inject it into this already bloodthirsty animal, the animal will immediately become one hundred times hungrier and more bloodthirsty than normal!"

"A total waste of time," COBRA Commander insists. "But go ahead, Bludd—show me I'm wrong!"

The guards drag the alligator up to Torpedo and Trip-Wire, who stare at it helplessly. The animal nearly breaks away from the guards, but they hold tight. Major Bludd prepares to inject the serum into the struggling creature.

You realize you have no choice. It is time to act—*now*! "*Attack!*" you cry.

Turn to page 71.

No one is better at dodging enemy weapon-fire than Wild Bill. The *Dragonfly* whirls and drops, then picks up altitude and spins away from the attacking fighters.

"Back at 'em!" you cry. "Let's ruin their morning!"

Wild Bill quickly obliges. "A little missilefire might make 'em wish they were back home scrambling some eggs," he says, activating the powerful helicopter's missile launchers.

"Fire One!" you cry.

Wild Bill pushes a red button. The first missile speeds toward its black and red COBRA target with a whoooosh.

A hit!

The COBRA jet explodes in a blaze of yellow and white flames. You watch as fiery pieces of debris drop to the swamps below.

But you have momentarily forgotten that there were *two* COBRA attack jets. The remaining one has taken the opportunity to position itself behind you.

"Spin around! Spin around!" you cry to Wild Bill. But you realize that you may be too late....

Turn to page 36.

Carrying the explosive device, Deep Six plunges into the cold Atlantic waters. You watch on the scanner as he descends into the ocean's depths. Down, down he dives, one man against an entire fortress.

Your mind cannot keep out the doubts as you watch Deep Six dive closer and closer to the spot where he will plant the underwater bomb. How long will the freighter's antiradar shield keep you from being spotted by the COBRAs below? Do they already know you're there? Are they setting a trap? Has Deep Six risked his life for nothing?

Suddenly Cutter's voice breaks into your thoughts. "Uh-oh," he says, pointing to the scanner screen. "Looks like Deep Six has company."

You look at the screen in alarm. Deep Six has company, all right. *Sharks!*

. . . .
Go on to page 63.

"How many are there?" you ask, your voice trembling as you stare at the screen.

"Only two," Cutter replies.

"Two is enough!" you say. You watch as Deep Six continues his descent, the sharks darting back and forth above him. "They're just circling him. They haven't attacked—yet," you say.

"We'd better send someone down to help him out," Cutter suggests.

"I'll go," Lady Jaye declares, grabbing a specially designed protective diving suit before anyone can protest. "I'll take my laser automatic. It'll work underwater. Those sharks are dead meat!"

"Wait!" Recondo protests. "In the jungle we know that most animals won't attack if you don't give them cause. Deep Six seems to be gettin' to where he wants to go. I think we should leave him on his own."

You stare at the screen, watching Deep Six dive down toward the COBRA fortress with the sharks swimming above his head.

Cutter looks at you. "Which will be it, Wiseguy?"

If you decide to let Lady Jaye dive down and blast the sharks, turn to page 11.

If you decide to let Deep Six continue his descent alone, turn to page 43.

"*Halt!*" the leader of the Crimson Guards commands.

Stoney steps forward proudly, gesturing toward you, his prisoners, with his rifle. "Mission accomplished, sir," he calls to the Crimson Guard leader. "I guess we did pretty good for fishermen, huh?"

"*Step back, fool!*" the Crimson Guard lieutenant yells angrily.

This is not the reaction Stoney expected from his employer. He takes a step back uncertainly. The other fishermen stand frozen, their rifles at their sides.

"We have orders to destroy the G.I. Joe Team," the Crimson Guard leader tells Stoney.

"Well...uh...fine. That ain't my business, I'm sure," Stoney stammers. "You just hired me and the boys to capture 'em and—"

The COBRAs raise their rifles.

"And I'm sorry to inform you that COBRA Commander doesn't want any witnesses," he tells Stoney. "So we have orders to kill you, too!"

Turn to page 80.

The battle continues. The fishermen put up a better fight than you would have imagined. Did you make the right decision to stand and fight them?

Finally you drive them back. As the fishermen retreat into the dense tangle of swamp trees, you think maybe you did make the right decision. "I *knew* we could take 'em!" Gung-Ho cries happily, firing a rifle into the air in celebration.

But you quickly realize there is little cause for celebration. The fishermen have run off. But Cutter is badly wounded, shot in the abdomen. And Recondo has been shot in the leg.

"You've got to complete the mission," Cutter tells you, his voice weak from pain. "Leave us here. Go after Torpedo and Trip-Wire. You can pick us up after you rescue them."

"*If* we rescue them," you say. You realize your mission will be a lot harder to accomplish without two of your team members, especially without Recondo and his knowledge of the jungle.

But you've got to try....

Turn to page 20.

"Through the swamps!" you cry to Trip-Wire. "Let's see what this baby can do over rough terrain!"

KA-RRROOOOOM!

The *Water Moccasin*s launch a barrage of weaponfire. Birds cry out and shrieking animals flee as you try to outrace the COBRAs.

The new Hovercraft floats over the swamps as Trip-Wire maneuvers it, twisting and turning, sliding through the narrow openings between trees, splashing over deep water inlets as you attempt to lose your pursuers.

"We're doing it!" you cry happily, gazing into the view screen as the COBRA Hovercrafts sink back farther and farther. "We're doing it! We're—"

The Hovercraft stalls, sputters, stops.

"We're—doomed...."

"Stalled out," Trip-Wire says, shaking his head. "It did this the other day, too. I guess there are still a few bugs to be worked out."

COBRA *Water Moccasin*s surround you. You have no choice but to surrender. If there are bugs to be worked out of the new Hovercraft, COBRA will have to do it. For you, the test drive—and the adventure—have stalled.

THE END

"Okay—let 'er blow!" you yell.

"But the charge is only halfway down!" Shipwreck calls down.

"You heard me! Let 'er blow!" you scream angrily. You know that if you've been spotted by COBRA, every second counts.

You throw yourself flat on the deck and wait for the explosion, unable to stop the questions racing through your mind. Will the freighter be able to withstand the force of the blast? How much damage will the explosion do to the fortress? And what's going to happen to Trip-Wire and Torpedo if they're down there?

BA-RRRRRROOOOOOOOOMMMMM!

Turn to page 50.

"This whole thing makes me angrier than a hungry gator!" Gung-Ho declares, leaping to his feet. "Those swamps are gonna shake when I get down there—'cause I'm gonna shake some heads together!"

"Uh-oh! Better tie him down! The ragin' Cajun is at it again!" Deep Six says, giving the scowling Gung-Ho a playful rap on the shoulder.

Gung-Ho gets on your nerves sometimes, and he takes a lot of ribbing for being so ... gung ho—but you wouldn't want to go on a mission like this without him.

A few moments later the whir of chopper blades breaks the silence of the night. "Let's go get 'em!" you yell as you and your team members pile into Wild Bill's big copter.

"You want smoking or nonsmoking?" Wild Bill asks, climbing into the cockpit.

"My guns are gonna be smokin' when we get down there!" Gung-Ho cries over the roar of the *Dragonfly*'s engine.

The chopper lifts off. Up, up into the night sky you whir, south toward Florida—and toward the unknown....

Turn to page 56.

BA-RRRRROOOOOOOM!

COBRA's antiship missiles blow you from the waters.

Sometimes *waiting* is the riskiest action of all!

THE END

You and your five companions leap out from behind the trees and burst into the camp, your rifles blazing. The COBRA guards are caught by surprise. One falls, then another.

You pull out your knife and slash at the ropes that hold Torpedo and Trip-Wire to the post.

"Way to go!" Trip-Wire yells, pulling free. All three of you dive to the ground as COBRA rifles ring out a deadly counterattack.

You look up to see Gung-Ho battling three COBRA soldiers at once. "Get COBRA Commander!" you yell. But you see that you are too late. As Jaye races after them, COBRA Commander and the Baroness flee into the *Water Moccasin* and speed away.

The COBRA soldiers have regained the advantage. You continue to fight, but you are surrounded and outnumbered. You've got to come up with a plan—fast!

Think fast and turn to page 87.

"This trip may be dangerous," you tell Stoney. "We don't want to involve anyone we don't have to."

Stoney scratches at the tangles of his matted red hair. "You turnin' me down?" he asks, staring hard at you.

"We'll set out on our own," you say firmly. "Recondo is at home in any jungle."

Stoney spits on the ground and turns away in disgust. The other fishermen also turn and walk away, slowly heading back to their small shacks.

"Which way, Recondo?" you ask.

Recondo squints at the line of low trees that forms the edge of the jungle. "Straight ahead, I guess, till we find some clues. The jungle always offers up clues."

"I've got a *clue* for you," a voice snaps. "You ain't goin' anywhere!" You turn to discover Stoney and the other fishermen standing in a line. Instead of fishing poles, they're now carrying automatic rifles!

Turn to page 18.

The other fishermen return to their huts as Stoney leads you into the Everglades. The trees are twisted and stooped, and sometimes the narrow path falls under two or three feet of stagnant water, which you tromp through, your eyes alert, your mind racing ahead to what you will do when you arrive at the COBRA camp.

You walk for hours, but you cover little ground. The treacherous terrain takes all of your concentration. Your tall, bearded guide walks quickly, confidently, and silently ahead of you past beds of sleeping alligators, through clumps of weeds that tower over your heads and over deep pits of wet sand in which you sink down to your knees.

Evening arrives wet and gray. Wisps of fog float under the bending trees. The fog grows thicker as you continue to walk. Night follows with its eerie animal sounds and whispering winds.

"*Hey—Stoney! Stoney!*" you call.

No reply.

"He's gone!" Lady Jaye calls through the darkness and fog. "He's deserted us here!"

Turn to page 2.

"I don't know how long our antiradar camouflage screen will keep COBRA from detecting us," Shipwreck warns. "If they have scanners that can get around it and they spot us, they'll blow us out of the water as easily as blowing out a match!"

"I have an idea," Cutter says, still staring at the huge structure revealed on the radar screen. "We can drop a depth charge powerful enough to blast a big hole in the COBRA fortress, a hole big enough to drown them all down there."

"And we drown Torpedo and Trip-Wire along with the COBRAs?" you ask.

"No, no," Cutter says impatiently. "We just use the depth charge as a threat. We radio COBRA and we tell them we've dropped the depth charge. We tell them we'll activate it—unless they release our buddies and return the Hovercraft to us."

"Hmmm...it just might work," you say.

"Wait, I have a different strategy," Deep Six interrupts.

"Quickly—we may have already been spotted," you tell him.

Turn to page 29.

74

"We're picking up a lot of water!" Lady Jaye calls up to you. "The COBRAs have knocked a pretty good hole back here!"

Trip-Wire straightens out the craft and guides it out into deeper waters, swerving away from COBRA gunfire. But the COBRAs know they have you. Their four vehicles surround your Hovercraft. They begin to close in tighter and tighter, bringing their *Water Moccasins* closer.

"This thing has guns in the front and side," Trip-Wire explains. "But there's no way we can knock out all four *Water Moccasins* at once!"

"We may go down—but we'll let 'em know they've been in a fight!" you vow.

Wait—what is that sound from portside? Sounds like weaponfire!

Turn to page 33.

"Okay, Bludd," you hear COBRA Commander say menacingly, "show me why you dragged us to this detestable swamp!"

"It will be a pleasure," Major Bludd sneers. "You won't be sorry you came."

COBRA Commander swats at a mosquito. "Make it quick, Bludd. What are these prisoners doing here?"

Bludd laughs. "These two fools stumbled into our camp," he says, jabbing Torpedo with the nose of his rifle. "They seemed completely unaware that we have been performing experiments down here. Of course, we cannot let them leave and tell their superiors about our little tests. Instead, we will have them participate! Ha ha!"

Bludd signals to four guards. The guards drag forward a gigantic alligator on a chain!

Turn to page 59.

"GERONIMOOOOOO!"

You leap out of the *Dragonfly* and drop through the red sky. Your parachute opens, catches the wind, and you float.

You were first out of the chopper, so you cannot see your companions. But you know they are in the air, parachuting down to the swamp with you.

Down, down you float ... down into the largest alligator bed in the Florida swamps!

You watch helplessly as the gigantic creatures wait for you to land. Does it appear to you that they are smiling? Why, of course they are. How often do such tasty visitors drop in for breakfast?!?

THE END

"Only five or six guards. The rest of 'em are asleep," Gung-Ho whispers. "Let's go get 'em. This is going to be more fun than a Louisiana hayride!"

"Not so fast," you whisper back. "We don't even know if Torpedo and Trip-Wire are here."

"Let me sneak into the camp and do a little spying," Recondo says. "You wait back here. No sense in attacking this camp if our buddies aren't here."

"It *always* makes sense to attack COBRAs!" Gung-Ho insists, raising his rifle.

"Down, boy, down!" Cutter says, pulling him back.

"Maybe we *should* attack now," Lady Jaye suggests. "If Recondo sneaks into the camp and gets caught, we'll lose the element of surprise."

It's up to you to decide the strategy, Wiseguy.

Attack the camp now? Turn to page 30.

Send Recondo to see if your buddies are in the camp? Turn to page 81.

79

The Crimson Guards raise their rifles and await the command to fire. The G.I. Joe Team is trapped in the middle—between the COBRA Guard and the armed fishermen. The ocean is on one side of you, dense swampland vegetation on the other. There is no time for strategy. There is only time to *act*.

"Tackle 'em!" you cry, and you turn and lunge at one of the startled fishermen, grabbing him around the knees and pulling him down to the sand.

COBRA rifles ring out as the others follow your example. In the confusion that follows, you hear Stoney utter a final cry of agony when a COBRA bullet hits its mark. His rifle flies out of his hand. You grab it and turn it on the COBRAs.

The other members of the Joe Team have wrested rifles away from the fishermen, and the jungle echoes with the roar of automatic gunfire. You roll under the cover of a log that has washed ashore, firing Stoney's rifle at the leader of the Crimson Guard. But the rifle jams. You toss it aside. It's clear that you are outnumbered and outgunned. You realize that your hopes have just about gone with that jammed rifle.

The COBRAs move in for the kill....

Turn to page 23.

"Okay, Recondo—you've got the job," you say. "Get in there and get out. See what you can find out—but don't take any risks."

"Me? Take risks?" he asks, grinning.

"If you're not back in an hour, we're coming in after you," you tell him. But he is already treading his way through the thick trees, circling to the back of the small camp, well away from the light of the glowing campfires.

The Joe Team rests behind the low, rustling trees, but you find it impossible to sleep. Your mind is with Recondo, darting through the shadows. You listen carefully, but you hear only the wind and the low calls of the Everglades' night creatures.

You glance at your watch every few minutes. Nearly an hour has passed. Where is Recondo? You decide to give him five more minutes before you begin rescue operations.

"I'm back," a voice beside you whispers.

"Recondo!" you say. "Did you find them?"

"Oh, I found them all right, but not in this camp." Seeing your puzzled looks, he explains. "We've been observing a decoy. Our buddies are in another camp a couple of miles back. And I don't think we should go in there right away. Trip-Wire and Torpedo are in mighty strange company."

"Like who?" Cutter asks.

Recondo stares at the ground. "Like Major Bludd," he answers. "Bludd and a pen full of giant alligators."

Turn to page 41.

Sure enough, another Hovercraft is roaring toward you over the dark ocean waves. "Let's take it," Gung-Ho says.

"Wait!" you say, holding him back from the gun turret. "Look at the markings on the side. That's not a COBRA craft!"

Hands wave at you from the approaching Hovercraft. It pulls up alongside the *Whale*, and Torpedo and Trip-Wire poke their heads out. "Hey—are we in Hawaii yet? This island boy wants to go home!" Trip-Wire yells, a big grin on his face.

"That explosion knocked a good hole in the COBRA fortress. They completely forgot about us, they were so desperate to get into their Hovercrafts and escape," Torpedo explains. "So we grabbed back this test boat and did a little escaping of our own!"

"It was real easy," Trip-Wire adds happily.

"Yeah, easy," you say, not exactly agreeing. "And now comes the hard part."

"What's that, Wiseguy?" Cutter asks.

"Explaining to Duke how we somehow managed to blow up our own freighter! Uh...maybe you and Trip-Wire could explain that part, whaddaya say, Torpedo? Hey—Torpedo?!"

But Torpedo and Trip-Wire have roared away in their test craft. Like you, they'd rather face a COBRA army than an angry Duke!

THE END

82

A battered sign beside the narrow road through the Arizona desert reads: SILVER SPRINGS, POP. 320. As you pull into the tiny mining town, you realize it must be an old sign. The springs obviously dried up many years before, and the town dried up with it. But it is the only town between Tucson and the site of the COBRA radio transmission.

You see a small general store with a gas pump in the back and a few shacks that may or may not be deserted. You and your fellow team members climb out of your jeeps and, warily watching for any sign of life on the deserted street, walk into the general store.

An old man with a white stubble of a beard stands hunched behind the dusty counter. He doesn't bother to look up, even though you're probably his only customers of the day.

"Excuse me," you say, stepping up to the counter. He still doesn't look up. "We're looking for some buddies. You see any soldiers come through here recently?"

"Can't say as I have," the old man slowly replies, staring down at his empty counter.

"Would you tell us if you *did* see 'em?" Gung-Ho asks impatiently.

"Can't say," the store owner mumbles.

You place a ten-dollar bill on the counter and watch the old man's eyes light up. "Think this might help your memory?" you ask.

....

Turn to page 4.

83

You turn to Recondo, just to be sure. "You could lead us through this swamp, couldn't you?" you ask.

Recondo grins. "A piece of cake," he says. "But finding the COBRA camp is another matter. It could be hidden anywhere. It could take us days to find it."

"And so you think we should—"

"Pay him," Recondo interrupts. "Terrain like this is my second home. I wouldn't mind spending weeks in the swamp. But we don't have weeks."

"Okay," you say, grateful that Duke gave you a generous expense account for this mission. You turn to Stoney. "Five hundred dollars takes us to the COBRA camp."

"Money in advance," Stoney says, spitting on the sand and stretching out a gnarled, bony hand. You count out five one-hundred-dollar bills and place them in the outstretched hand.

"You just hired yourself a guide," Stoney says. "The best swamp guide that ever roamed the backwaters and—"

"We don't have time for you to be colorful," you tell him. "Just shut up and take us to where we have to go."

Turn to page 73.

84

Furious, Major Bludd cries out and lunges toward you, the syringe still in his hand. You dodge out of his way. He stumbles forward—right into the jaws of the alligator. Despite the heat, chills run through you as you hear his screams.

A few seconds later you and the other team members have all made it safely into the gigantic Hovercraft. "How do you work this thing?" you ask, staring hopelessly at the complicated control panel.

"Nothing to it," Trip-Wire says, stumbling over you to get to the controls. A few seconds later the Hovercraft is racing away. "Oh, no," Trip-Wire says suddenly, peering into a view screen. "They're following us in a COBRA *Ferret*!"

Oh, no is *right*! The *Ferret* is an all-terrain tank—armed with missiles!

Turn to page 25.

"Okay, let's go, I guess," you say, reluctantly climbing into the sleek new Hovercraft. "The second test drive has *got* to be better than the first—right?"

"Definitely," Torpedo agrees with a smile.

As you watch the others take off in the *Whale*, you realize that Torpedo is still hunched over the controls. "Now," he mutters, "how do you start this thing? Is it the thingamajig or the doohickey? I never can remember...."

THE END

An idea forms suddenly! You see the experimental Hovercraft on the other side of the camp. "It's immense!" you tell yourself. "We could all fit into it easily!" But can you all get to it?

In the midst of the fighting the guards struggle to keep control of the alligator. It snaps and claws at the ground. Perhaps if you freed the alligator, it would turn on its COBRA captors. And cutting the alligator free might create enough of a diversion to let you and your backup get to the Hovercraft.

· ·

What will you do? Order the Joe Team to make a run for the experimental Hovercraft now? Turn to page 3.

Take the time to create a diversion by setting the alligator free? Turn to page 19.

You train your guns on the struggling COB-RAs, but they are not prepared to give you a fight. One raises an automatic rifle and tries to fire it at you, but the gun is waterlogged and he tosses it away with a sigh of defeat.

"Hey—do we have to swim back to The Pit, or are you guys gonna give us a lift?"

You recognize Torpedo's voice immediately. He and Trip-Wire are swimming up to the freighter.

"Very glad to see you," Trip-Wire calls up to you. "Very glad to see *anyone*!"

You pull them up onto the deck of the freighter. "What were you guys *doin'* down there anyway?" Gung-Ho asks, shaking his head.

"Well, we weren't diving for pearls, I'll tell you that!" Trip-Wire replies, shuddering from the cold.

"Let's get moving," Torpedo says eagerly.

"Aren't we forgetting something?" you ask him. "A little something like an experimental Hovercraft worth a few hundred million dollars?"

"Oh—that hunk of junk?" Torpedo says. "We ditched it on the shore just before we were captured. It goes about as well as a '48 Studebaker! Even COBRA wasn't interested in it!"

"Well...for some reason, people in Washington are interested in it," you say with a grin. "Let's go pick it up. Then we can call this pleasure cruise over!"

THE END

TA-116